S0-CMS-820

# THE SPIDER

## and Other Stories by Carl Ewald

# THE SPIDER

## and Other Stories by Carl Ewald

---

Translated by

EVA LE GALLIENNE

Illustrated by Bill Woodman

Thomas Y. Crowell · New York

For information address Thomas Y. Crowell, 10 East 53rd Street,
New York, N.Y. 10022. Published simultaneously in Canada by
Fitzhenry & Whiteside Limited, Toronto.
Designed by Amelia Lau

---

**Library of Congress Cataloging in Publication Data**
Ewald, Carl, 1856–1908.
The spider, and other stories.
SUMMARY: A collection of short stories by the
19th-century Danish author.
1. Children's stories, Danish. [1. Short
stories] I. Le Gallienne, Eva, 1899– II.
Woodman, Bill. III. Title.
PZ7.E946Sp 1980 [Fic] 79–8043
ISBN 0–690–04042–3
ISBN 0–690–04043–1 (lib. bdg.)

10 9 8 7 6 5 4 3 2 1
First Edition

# CONTENTS

# *The Spider*

The fence had started to give way under the weight of the trees and bushes that had grown up around it, so they had to be cut down. Only the stumps remained, but they were still alive, and pretty soon they were covered with long, spindly new shoots.

In among the tree stumps many plants flourished: Tansy, Wild Parsley, and other things as well. They were all very much alike, and people who didn't know the difference simply called them weeds. But they were very vain; they grew tall, expanded, stretched out their branches, and pretended to be bushes. Indeed, they almost persuaded themselves that they really *were* bushes. They quite forgot that they would wither and die at the first touch of frost and would have to start all over again the following spring from tiny seeds, just like the common Camomile or Heartsease; and if anyone reminded them of it they pretended not to hear, or refused to listen, or simply denied the whole thing outright.

Some of them had pretty white flowers which they held proudly aloft like parasols; they regarded the young Shoots from the stumps and bushes as so many overgrown children who could produce neither flower nor fruit.

"Why, it's a regular forest!" exclaimed the Fieldmouse one evening as she gazed up at the green leaves with clear, shining eyes.

"Of course! We *are* the forest," said the Tansy.

"Take a look around," said the Wild Parsley. "If we appeal to you, why not build a nest in our branches? We'll put everything we have at your disposal."

"Don't listen to them," the young Shoots cried. "Let them brag while it's still summer. By autumn they'll be gone; there'll be nothing left of them."

"Autumn? What's autumn?" said the Tansy.

"There's no such thing as autumn," said the Wild Parsley, glaring at the young Shoots. "It's just a silly story made up to fool children like you."

"Still—autumn is a fact," said the Fieldmouse. "And after autumn comes winter; that's when you need a well-stocked larder. I'm glad you reminded me. I think I'll dig myself a little hole among the rocks and start collecting my supplies."

"If a hole in the ground appeals to you—suit yourself!" said the Tansy.

"We aspire to higher things," said the Wild Parsley.

They were silent for a while, deep in thought. Then the Wild Parsley heaved a sigh and put their thoughts into words: "Oh! If only a little bird would come and build her nest in our branches!" she cried.

"Yes, yes!" said the Tansy. "We'd rock its nest so gently and shield it from the hot rays of the sun, and it would be so delighted with us that all the genuine bushes would wither away with envy."

"Would you care to try me?" asked a voice.

An odd-looking gray creature came craw along the fence.

"Who are you?" asked the Wild Parsley.

"I am the Spider," the creature answered.

"Can you fly?" asked the Tansy.

"I can do a bit of everything at a pinch."

"Do you eat flies?" asked the Wild Parsley.

"All day long."

"Do you lay eggs?" asked the Tansy. "For I suppose you are a female?"

"Yes—thank God!" said the Spider.

"Then you're the bird for us," said the Wild Parsley.

"A hearty welcome to you," said the Tansy. "You don't look very heavy, so there'll be no danger of broken branches."

"Go ahead and build as soon as you like," said the Wild Parsley. "You'll find plenty of material along the fence."

"And if you run short we can always spare a leaf or two," said the Tansy.

"Thank you; I always carry my own materials," said the Spider.

"You don't seem to have any luggage," said the Tansy.

"I daresay your husband is bringing it later," said the Wild Parsley.

"Thank God, I have no husband," said the Spider.

"Why, you poor thing!" said the Fieldmouse, who had been listening intently. "How sad and lonely you must be!"

"The usual female twaddle," said the Spider. "It's just that kind of talk that makes us women so silly and contemptible. 'My husband this, my husband that'—there's no end to it! Why on earth should one want a husband anyhow? They're just a pain and a nuisance. If, by some remote chance, I ever took a husband, I certainly wouldn't let him live with me."

"What a way to talk!" said the Fieldmouse. "I'd be absolutely miserable if my husband didn't live with me. And how could I ever possibly manage all the children without his help? The dear, good soul!"

"Please don't mention children," answered the Spider. "All that petting and cuddling disgusts me. You simply lay your eggs in a good practical spot, and the rest is up to them."

"She doesn't talk like a bird," said the Wild Parsley thoughtfully.

"I'm beginning to be a bit doubtful about her too," said the Tansy.

"Call me whatever you like," said the Spider. "In any event, I never associate with other birds, so if there are too many around here I shan't stay."

"Good gracious," said the Wild Parsley, who was afraid they might lose her, "scarcely any birds come here."

"When the trees were cut down they all flew off to the forest," said the Tansy.

"Yes, it's sad here now," said the young Shoots. "You never hear bird songs anymore."

"It's just right here," said the Spider. "I hear a lot of flies buzzing—that pleases me."

"Whenever you feel like building, we're ready," said the Wild Parsley and the Tansy; and they drew themselves up to their full height.

The Spider crawled about on a tour of inspection, and the Fieldmouse followed her with her eyes.

"Forgive my asking," she said, "but if you believe in letting your eggs fend for themselves, why bother to build a nest for them?"

"Now, listen to me, little Mousey," said the Spider. "You'd better realize once and for all that I am an independent woman. I'm thoroughly capable of looking after my own affairs. And if I should ever condescend to take some little runt of a husband, all I can say is, he'd better look after *his.*"

"How you talk!" said the Mouse. "*My* husband is twice as big and four times as strong as I am."

"I've never met him," said the Spider indifferently. "In my family, the men aren't even a quarter as big as we are. A lot of weaklings not worth a fly. I'd think twice before sharing my home with such a puny creature. Well—now I must start building."

"It's getting dark; hadn't you better wait till morning?" said the Wild Parsley.

"What are you going to build with?" asked the Tansy.

"I prefer the dark," said the Spider, "and, as I told you, I carry my own materials."

She then climbed to the very top of the Tansy and surveyed the landscape.

"You must have good eyes if you can see in the dark," said the Mouse. "Mine are nothing to scoff at, but I shouldn't care to start building in this kind of light."

"Speaking of eyes, I have eight of them," said the Spider. "And they see all they have to. I may as well tell you I have eight legs too—so don't be surprised on that score. Altogether, I'm a woman used to making her own way in the world. I've had some close calls, but I've always managed. There's no nonsense about me."

With that she pressed her rear end down firmly on the branch she was sitting on, then flung herself headfirst into space.

"She'll break her neck!" cried the Mouse in terror.

"I have no neck," said the Spider from below. "And if I did have one, I shouldn't break it. Just you run home and cuddle up to your darling husband, and when you come back here in the morning you'll see what a clever woman can accomplish if she doesn't waste her time on a lot of sentimental love-making."

The Mouse went on her way. She had things to attend to, and, besides, the Spider had hurt her feelings. The Tansy and the Wild Parsley were, of course, obliged to remain—and the young Shoots too. They none of them got a wink of sleep all night long, for the Spider's behavior was so remarkable that they simply couldn't take their eyes off her.

"She *is* a bird," said the Wild Parsley happily.

"I suppose she must be," said the Tansy.

But the young Shoots gave them a scornful look. "She couldn't possibly be a bird," they said. "Can she sing? Have you heard her give so much as a single peep?"

The Wild Parsley and the Tansy looked at each other thoughtfully. And when the Spider stood still for a moment to catch her breath, the Wild Parsley asked cautiously, "Can you sing?"

"Pooh!" said the Spider. "Do you think I waste my time on that sort of rubbish? And, anyway, what is there to sing about? Life is a tough, grim business. If she's to succeed in this world, a single woman must put her shoulder to the wheel and keep pushing."

"Birds sing," said the Tansy.

"They sing because they're in love. I am not in love," said the Spider.

"Just you wait till the right one comes along," said the Wild Parsley.

"If he ever does come, he'd better look out," said the Spider.

At that she flung herself headfirst into space again, and continued to do so all night.

When dawn began to break, the Tansy and the Wild Parsley almost collapsed with amazement.

There, suspended in the space between their

branches, with her body hunched up and her legs drawn under her, sat the Spider, sound asleep.

"Is she perching on you?" asked the Tansy.

"No, she's not," answered the Wild Parsley. "I thought she was perching on you."

"She isn't," said the Tansy.

"She's not perching on us either," said the young Shoots.

"She *is* a bird," exclaimed the Wild Parsley and the Tansy with delight.

"A bird doesn't fall fast asleep in midair," said the young Shoots.

"She must be a magician," said the Mouse, who had turned up just at that moment. "Wait till the sun's up—then we'll be able to see better."

And the sun came up, and then they saw.

Between the stems of the Tansy and the Wild Parsley a number of the finest threads had been stretched; they crisscrossed each other, forming a lacy, circular web that sparkled in the sunshine. It was a beautiful sight. Other threads had been added to the basic pattern in ever-widening circles.

"Now I see," said the Mouse. "She was perching in the middle of *that* thing. But where is she now?"

"Here I am," the Spider said from underneath a leaf. "I don't like too much sunshine. What do you think of my work? Though, actually, it's not quite finished."

"I can't help thinking," said the Mouse, "that it's a very odd-looking nest."

"Nests—nests—nests!" said the Spider. "You're the one who started all this talk of nests. Do you take me for the kind of soft, sentimental, effeminate woman you are—and all the others? What use have I for a nest? I'm comfortable enough here under this leaf; it's pleasant and shady and quite good enough for me. That is my web—the web I catch my flies in. I think we're in for a little rain. I'll be able to get to work again and finish the job."

And, sure enough, in a little while the clouds began to gather, the sun went in, and a mild, gentle rain started to fall. As soon as it had stopped, the Spider came out from under her leaf, stretched her eight legs contentedly in the damp air, and went to work.

They all watched in amazement as she produced quantities of fine threads out of her abdomen. These she proceeded to comb out with tiny combs she carried at the end of her claws; she then twisted them into a single strong strand and attached it to the web wherever she thought it seemed weak or had too wide an opening. The threads were sticky and greasy so that no fly could possibly escape. Toward the end of the day the web was finished, and everyone gazed at it in wonder.

"Now I'm in business," said the Spider.

Just then a Starling came and perched at the top of one of the young tree Shoots.

"Anything to eat around here?" he asked. "A grub or two, or perhaps even a spider?"

The Tansy and the Wild Parsley remained silent; they almost withered with fright at the thought of losing their lodger. The Mouse ran off—she was afraid she might give the show away—but the young Shoots with one accord announced that a fine fat spider had arrived the day before and had already woven her web.

"I don't see any sign of her," said the Starling, and he flew away.

With lightning speed the Spider had dropped to earth on a long thread and lain motionless, as though dead. Now she crept up again and settled herself, with her eight legs outstretched, in the middle of her web.

"That was a close call," she said. "Now it's my turn."

A dainty little fly soon came along; it didn't see the web, flew right into it, was caught, and hung there pitifully.

"That's the ticket," said the Spider.

She bit it with her mandibles. They were full of poison, and it died immediately. Then she ate it. She did the same with the next three that were caught in the web. By then she'd had enough. An assortment of tiny insects had meanwhile strayed into her web, but she paid no attention to them. She waited till a really large, juicy fly turned up. She stung it to death, spun some threads around it like a little sack, and carefully hung it up.

"I'll save him. He'll be a nice morsel for a rainy day," she said.

"Very sensible," said the Mouse. "That's the first thing you've said that I heartily agree with. But I must say I don't like your methods. They strike me as treacherous. Fancy using poison like the vipers! I think that's disgusting!"

"Do you indeed!" said the Spider scornfully. "Is it any worse than what everyone else does? I suppose you sound an alarm or blow a trumpet before you attack your prey, don't you, Mousey dear?"

"It wouldn't matter if I did—that is, if I *had* a trumpet," said the Mouse. "Thank God I'm not like you—I'm no murderer. I gather my nuts, or my seeds, or anything else of that sort that comes my way. I've never harmed a living soul."

"No, you're just a sweet little old-fashioned girl," said the Spider. "You're grateful for the little you have and make the best of it. Then you trot home to your darling husband and your precious children. Well—I'm made of different stuff. All that lovey-dovey nonsense means nothing to me. But I *do* have an appetite, and I crave meat—lovely, juicy fly meat. And a lot of it. I ask no one for anything; whatever I need I get for myself. If things go well, I have the satisfaction of knowing it's all my own doing. If things go badly, you won't catch me whining or complaining to anyone. It's a pity there aren't a lot more women like me."

"How crude you are," said the Mouse.

"Fiddle-faddle," said the Spider. "People are all

the same. I'm no worse than anybody else. Take the Tansy and the Wild Parsley here: Do you suppose they don't quarrel over every butterfly and bee and do their best to steal each other's light and air?"

"Very true," said the Wild Parsley.

"She's a wise woman," said the Tansy.

"And then you have such an ugly name," said the Mouse.

"I can't help that," said the Spider. "I was given the name because of the little drop of poison I carry in my mandibles.* People are such sentimental hypocrites! They're overcome with pity for all the poor little flies I catch. But just let a fly land on the end of one of their noses! They kill flies all the time. I don't particularly want to change my name, but you can call me Spinner if you like. A sweet little lady mouse like you can surely say *that* without a qualm. Besides, it suits me. No other creature in the world can spin as well as I can."

"That may be all very well," said the Mouse, shaking her head, "but your behavior is not respect-

*The literal translation of *Edderkop* (the Danish for spider) is "poison-cup."

able. And then you *look* so unattractive."

"So that's it, is it!" answered the Spider with a laugh. "Doesn't it occur to you, dear little Madame Mouse, that my costume is highly practical? My simple gray dress suits my type of work perfectly; it doesn't attract attention, you see. Thank God I don't have to strut about in a lot of finery, hoping to catch a husband or snare a lover, as some women do. They're a disgrace to our sex, that's all I can say of them. Fools naturally despise me for wearing such plain clothes. Well, let them! What do I care for fools? I eat them when they happen to stray into my web."

The Mouse shook her head and went on her way. The Tansy and the Wild Parsley put their heads together and conversed in low tones. The Spider sat in the center of her web, stretched out her legs, and digested her meal. When the sun came out again, she crept into the shade under her leaf.

The Mouse came back and glanced up at the web. "Where is she? Is she asleep?" she asked.

"I think so," said the Wild Parsley. "Mind you don't wake her up with your silly chatter."

"Don't forget she is our bird," said the Tansy.

"She may be different from other birds, but she's had enough faith in us to honor us by building in our branches. We must insist that she be treated with respect."

"A fine bird *she* is!" scoffed the young Shoots.

"At any rate, she's a great deal better than nothing," said the Wild Parsley.

"Overgrown louts like you should keep their mouths shut," said the Tansy. "I don't see anyone building anything in you!"

"She's certainly not a bird," said the Mouse, "but there may be good in her all the same. In my opinion, she's a disappointed old maid. She's had an unhappy love affair. Just you mark my words, her lover jilted her. That hurts, you know. My first husband ran off with a white mouse just after the children were born, so I speak from experience."

"It's quite possible," said the Wild Parsley thoughtfully. "But what's to be done about it?"

"We must try to make her happy," said the Mouse. "We can't let her go on living this solitary life, growing more and more bitter every day. She'll lose all trace of womanly feeling and become hard as nails. We've simply got to find her a husband."

"If we only could!" said the Wild Parsley.

"Then perhaps she'd build a proper nest and lay eggs in it," said the Tansy.

"She might even sing to her babies," said the Wild Parsley.

"Then those stuck-up Bushes would have nothing on us," said the Tansy.

Just then the Spider stuck her head out from under her leaf. "What are you talking about?" she said.

"We were talking about you," said the Mouse. "We were saying that you really ought to get married. It's not good for a woman to remain single. She becomes sour and eccentric. Imagine the joy of having your own little babies to cherish and care for!"

"Rubbish," said the Spider.

"I don't care what you say, it's against nature," said the Mouse. "I shall certainly see what I can do for you. Every day on my way back and forth along the fence I meet many gentlemen Spiders. They're smaller than you are, it's true, but some of them look very nice. With luck I might even come across a large one. I intend to tell them that I know of a

lovely maiden lady who is simply longing for a suitor."

"Then you'd be telling a shocking lie," said the Spider. "And it's no good trying to find a large one. All our menfolk are weak, wretched little runts. No one has the slightest respect for them. You see, we discovered long ago that it's only women who amount to anything."

"I'll run along," said the Mouse. "I'll find the right one, never fear. I'm convinced that you'll be a happier and more agreeable creature once you fall in love."

"Yes! Just you run along, Mousey dear," said the Spider. "No man living could ever please me. But your little head is filled with nothing but sentimental nonsense."

With that she killed a fly, spun a web for it, hung it up, and disappeared under her leaf. The Mouse trotted off, and the Wild Parsley and the Tansy softly discussed the future.

Early the next morning a nice-looking gentleman Spider sat on a branch of the Wild Parsley, but at a safe distance from the ferocious maiden lady.

His claws were nicely polished, and he had spun

a couple of beautiful threads to prove his cleverness. He stretched himself and flexed his legs to show off his fine form. Seven of his eyes radiated love, while the eighth kept a sharp lookout lest she should try to eat him.

"Permit me, dear lady, to offer you my hand and my heart," he said.

"He expresses himself well," said the Wild Parsley.

"A delightful man," said the Tansy.

"Guff," said the Spider.

But the gentleman Spider was not put off so easily. Making a neat bow, he now focused two of his eyes on possible danger while redoubling the ardor of the other six. "Believe me, I would never be a burden to you," he said. "I have my own web a short way down the fence, and I am certainly capable of catching the few flies I have need of. As a matter of fact, I have five fat, juicy ones hanging in my larder now. It will be an honor to offer them to you, as proof that my wooing is prompted by love alone."

"Are you crazy?" said the Spider. "What use would I have for a weakling like you?"

"Good gracious," he said, and now only *one* of his

eyes radiated love, for she looked so very grim. "If my courtship is so offensive to you, I'll retire at once and await a more favorable opportunity."

"That would be wise of you," she said. "Now get out of here fast before I—"

He was on the ground in a flash, and she went after him. But he managed to escape, and shortly afterward she was in the center of her web again, looking sourer and more disagreeable than ever.

"What a woman!" said the Mouse.

"Yes—precisely!" said the Spider.

"It's perhaps as well not to take the first one that comes along," said the Wild Parsley.

"He just wasn't the right one," said the Tansy.

The unfortunate wooer ran from one end of the fence to the other telling all the gentlemen Spiders about the extraordinary maiden lady who had spun her web between the Wild Parsley and the Tansy. "She's as big as *this,*" he said, spreading out his eight legs as far as he could get them to go. "I've never seen anything more beautiful. But she's as proud as Satan. I'll never recover from her refusal. I've quite made up my mind now that I shall never marry."

They listened to his story with amazement and

wanted him to tell it over and over again. Before long the legend about the proud, beautiful Spider Princess had traveled all along the fence. After working hours, all the gentlemen Spiders gathered together to talk about her. Each one expressed his opinion at great length, and the more they discussed her, the more consumed with love they were. They agreed that life would scarcely be worth living without winning the hand of the legendary charmer.

One after another they went to woo, and all of them failed miserably.

The first one to make the attempt was a dashing fellow. On hearing the poor unfortunate wooer tell of offering the Princess the five flies he had hanging in his larder, he scoffed at him unmercifully. "Don't you know that women never pay attention to mere promises?" he said. "They demand cash down. Just you watch me."

He went to the Spider dragging a splendid bluebottle fly, and laid it at her feet without a word.

"Do you think I'd let myself be supported by a man?" she said.

Before he knew where he was, she had overpowered him and eaten him. She didn't touch the bluebottle; but later on, when she thought no one was looking, she ate that too.

The rest of the wooers fared no better.

Six of them she devoured while they were still in the middle of a sentence, and two of them didn't even get a chance to open their mouths. The Starling snapped one up just as he was making his initial bow; and another one fell into the ditch with terror when the Spider turned her eyes on him, and drowned there.

"That makes twelve," said the Mouse.

"I've lost count," said the Spider. "Perhaps now I'll have some peace."

"You are a dreadful woman," said the Mouse. "I predict that you will go childless to your grave."

For the first time, the Spider looked a little thoughtful.

"What a nuisance it is that one can't have children without having a man as well," she said.

"I believe her hard heart is beginning to soften," said the Mouse.

"Oh!" said the Wild Parsley.

"Ah!" said the Tansy.

"Rubbish," said the Spider.

But she continued to look thoughtful, contemplated her claws, and when a little fly flew into her web she never even noticed it. After a while she said:

"I suppose one really ought to bring a few capable girls into this world, if only to hand on a feeling of contempt for the males of the species. I can quite see that it might be one's duty."

"She's on the right path," whispered the Mouse. And the Tansy and the Wild Parsley nodded in agreement, but neither of them said anything for fear of interrupting the Spider's train of thought.

The Mouse scurried off along the fence and gathered all the surviving gentlemen Spiders together. "Whoever woos the Princess tomorrow morning will win her," she said. "She's quite changed. She has melted. Her heart is now like wax. She catches no flies, eats nothing, drinks nothing, just sits gazing wistfully into space. Hurry."

Then she scurried off again.

The gentlemen Spiders looked at one another thoughtfully. They remembered the fate of the eleven who had succumbed, and none of them had the courage to make the attempt. Two of them were even careful enough to creep under their respective leaves and hide, so as not to give way to temptation.

A few, however, remained to think over what the Mouse had said. Among them was a tiny, skinny, very young fellow who had always listened attentively to the stories of the legendary Princess but had never uttered a word.

"I think I'll have a try," he said suddenly.

"You?" shouted the others in unison.

And they started to laugh at the thought of this puny little upstart succeeding where so many fine gentlemen Spiders had given their lives.

But the little fellow let them laugh as much as they liked.

"I don't think I'm poaching on anyone else's preserve," he said quietly. "After all, none of you dares to try, and I'm willing to make the attempt. I've been over to have a look at her, and she certainly is a beautiful woman. She's rejected twelve; perhaps she'll accept the thirteenth. Anyway, I've an idea the courtship was never properly handled."

"Oh, you have, have you?" said the others, and they went on laughing. "And how do *you* propose to handle it?"

"Come and see for yourselves if you like," he said. "I'm going over to pay my court to her early tomorrow morning."

And that's just what he did.

Slowly and soberly, as though in deep thought, he crawled along the fence. The other gentlemen Spiders followed at a little distance. The young Shoots craned their necks to catch a glimpse of him. The Wild Parsley and the Tansy spread their blossoms and their leaves to the full to shelter him on his way. The Mouse stood on her hind legs and watched with eager curiosity.

The Princess sat in the middle of her web and pretended not to see him.

"Noble Princess," he said at last, "I have come to beg you to accept me as your husband."

"He's the thirteenth," she said to herself.

Still, she had to admit she liked him better than the others. They had all wanted to take her as a wife; this one begged her to accept him as a husband. It sounded so much nicer.

"She's going to give in!" said the Mouse as she danced with delight.

"Hush!" said the Wild Parsley.

"Quiet!" said the Tansy.

"She hasn't eaten him yet!" the other gentlemen Spiders cried.

"I know how presumptuous I am in making this request," said the wooer. "What's a mere man compared to a woman? And what has an insignificant little fellow like me to offer a splendid, magnificent lady like you?—you, the cleverest of women! But this is precisely what draws me to you."

She turned and looked at him.

He nearly sank into the ground with terror, and his eight eyes dropped before hers. All the other gentlemen Spiders rushed away in a panic.

"She's going to eat him now," said the Tansy and the Wild Parsley.

"Such a sweet girl!" said the young Shoots.

"She's a dreadful woman," said the Mouse.

But she didn't eat him.

She seized a fly that had just at that moment flown into her web, bit it to death, and slowly and carefully devoured it while observing him attentively.

What a weakling he looked, standing there shaking all over, thinking his last hour had come. But this was what she liked in him; it was fitting for a mere man, she thought.

As she showed no sign of attacking him, he recovered sufficiently to continue his speech. "I know only too well you couldn't possibly find me handsome," he said. "I don't claim to be any better than I am—just a poor male creature. But if I were fortunate enough to be the father of a daughter just like you, I should know I had not lived in vain. I would be humbly grateful all the rest of my days."

Then an amazing thing happened: She tore the leg off a fly and flung it to him, which in spider language is the same as saying "yes."

Trembling with joy and apprehension, he crept nearer to her.

"Very well," she said, "I'll take you. But be careful not to annoy me, for if you do I'll eat you."

"She's accepted him!" said the Mouse, swooning with delight.

"She's accepted him!" said the Tansy and the Wild Parsley.

"She's accepted him!" said the young Shoots, and they rustled with amazement.

"She's accepted him!" shouted the gentlemen Spiders, who had returned, but now took off again, partly to spread the news and partly to avoid being eaten at the wedding feast.

And what a wedding feast it was! All the inhabitants of the fence took part in the celebration. The Mouse was particularly pleased, since it was all her doing, but the Tansy and the Wild Parsley were happiest of all. Now a real family would make its home in their branches. Now they could be just as stuck-up as the real Bushes. Even the young Shoots were caught up in the general rejoicing and forgot to be sarcastic.

The wedding took place without delay; there was no reason to put it off. The Wild Parsley and the Tansy sprinkled their petals all about in honor of the festive occasion. The Mouse perched her children on the fence so that they might have a good look at the happy pair. The Harebells rang their chimes, the Poppies laughed, and the Morning Glories closed up half an hour earlier than usual, so as not to embarrass the newlyweds with ill-timed curiosity.

The bride ate all the flies she had in reserve without offering the bridegroom a single one. But it didn't matter, for he was so choked with happiness he couldn't have swallowed a morsel. He made himself as small as possible. Once she stroked his back with one of her combs, and he trembled so violently they all thought he would die.

Early the next morning, the Mouse was on the lookout.

"Have you seen anything of our young couple?" she asked.

"No," said the Wild Parsley.

"They're asleep," said the Tansy.

"What a blessing we managed to get her married at last!" said the Mouse. "You'll see how sweet and pliable she'll be. There's no end to the miracles love can perform. And then, when the babies start coming . . . !"

"Do you think then she'll sing?" asked the Tansy.

"Let us have faith that she will," said the Mouse. "She doesn't look like a singer to me, but, as I said before—the miracles of love! You'll see when she appears how radiant she'll be. We'll scarcely recognize her."

And the Mouse laughed with delight, and the Wild Parsley and the Tansy laughed, and the sun came up and laughed too.

Just then the Spider came crawling out from under her leaf.

"Congratulations!" squeaked the Mouse.

"Congratulations!" said the Tansy and the Wild Parsley.

The Spider stretched herself and yawned. Then she went and sat in the center of her web as though nothing had happened.

"May I ask how the dear husband is?" said the Mouse. "Perhaps he doesn't feel like getting up so early?"

"I ate him this morning," said the Spider.

The Mouse let out a shriek that was heard from one end of the fence to the other. The Tansy and the Wild Parsley trembled so that all their blossoms dropped off. The young Shoots creaked as though swept by a high wind.

"He looked so puny and silly sitting there beside me," said the Spider, "so I ate him. He should have stayed away from me."

"God have mercy on us all!" shrieked the Mouse.

"Eat her own beloved husband! How could she? How could she?"

"Alas!" said the Wild Parsley.

"Cry woe!" said the Tansy.

"Rubbish," said the Spider.

All that day it was very quiet along the fence, and the next day too.

The Spider guarded her web and caught and ate more flies than ever. She never said a word to anyone, and her eyes looked so fierce and wicked that no one dared say a word to her.

The gentlemen Spiders were careful to come nowhere near her. But they hastened to meet every evening to discuss the situation.

"After all, we must remember he *did* win her," said the most romantic of them.

The others all challenged him, demanding to know if he really thought it lucky to be eaten by one's bride the day after the wedding.

He didn't know how to answer that; his romanticism didn't go that far.

The Mouse crept in and out of her hole with bowed head. She felt as much concerned as though it had happened in her own family. The Tansy and the Wild Parsley let their parasols droop. They felt crestfallen and humiliated. They were sure the young Shoots would ridicule them unmercifully. But their defeat had been so devastating that the young Shoots felt quite sorry for them and, for once, decided to be kind.

One day when the sun beat down and the Spider had crept as far as possible into the shade of her leaf, the Wild Parsley bent over toward the Mouse's hole and whispered, "Psst! Little Mouse . . . !"

The Mouse stuck out her head. "What is it?" she asked.

"The Tansy and I want to ask you something," said the Wild Parsley. "You're so very clever—tell us what you think: Is it possible that a change might come over the Spider once she starts laying her eggs?"

"I think nothing about anything anymore," said the Mouse. "And I don't believe that dreadful woman could ever possibly lay any eggs."

But she did, all the same.

One fine morning she settled down to it and behaved in such a way that none of the creatures along the fence ever forgot it.

"Pooh!" she said. "To think one has to go through all this childbearing nonsense."

She laid a cluster of about twenty eggs and looked at them with disgust.

"You should build a nest for the eggs," said the Wild Parsley. "You know that all we have is at your disposal."

"Sit on them and hatch them out," said the Tansy. "We'll weave a roof over your head to protect you from the sun."

"You'd better collect lots of small flies for the children," said the Mouse. "You've no idea what a lot babies can eat."

"Why not practice singing them a lullaby?" said the young tree Shoots.

"Rubbish," said the Spider.

She laid four more egg clusters. Then she began to spin. Each egg cluster was separately encased in a pouchlike web of fine white threads, which she spun closely around them.

"She's not entirely devoid of feeling," said the Mouse.

The Spider took one of the egg clusters, crawled down the fence with it, and buried it in the ground.

WOODMAN

Then she climbed up again to fetch another; she kept this up until all five were safely buried.

"There! That's done!" she said. "That's the last time I'll ever go through *that* nonsense. Now, thank God, I'm a free, independent woman again!"

"A nice kind of woman, I must say!" said the Mouse. "I call her a disgrace to her sex!"

"She's such a sweet little bird!" said the young Shoots sarcastically.

The Tansy and the Wild Parsley were silent.

Next morning the Spider was nowhere to be seen.

"The Starling got her," said the Mouse. "One peck, and that was the end of her. I saw it with my own eyes."

"Hope she didn't give him indigestion," said the young Shoots. "She must have been a bitter beak-ful!"

Then autumn came, and winter.

The Mouse was snug in her hole, and the Spider's eggs were snug in the earth. The Tansy and the Wild Parsley withered and died. The young tree Shoots shed their leaves, but they withstood the storms of winter, and waited for the spring.

# *The Wind*

Monday morning the skipper stood up in his boat and swore. Then he spat into the water and swore again. He let out such a string of oaths that it was positively awful to listen to him.

"Here I've been a whole week waiting for an east wind," he said, "and all I get is one from the west. My fish are rotting in the hold. I'll be a ruined man. Listen to me, Wind! Turn around, damn you!"

"Can't, can't," answered the Wind sadly.

"You're a no-good, rotten wind!" said the skipper.

Tuesday morning all the blossoms on the old Apple Tree burst into bloom.

"This is the most important day in the year for me," said the Tree. "Today will decide my fate. Dear, darling Wind, don't blow today. Look at me! I'm in full bloom. If you blow my blossoms off I'll have no apples. So be a dear and stay quiet—just for today."

"I'd like nothing better," said the Wind, "if only I could." Then, suddenly, in a great gust, he swept over the tree, and all the lovely blossoms went whirling through the air.

"You're a cruel, mean wind!" said the Apple Tree.

Wednesday morning the miller stood outside his mill and looked up at the sky.

"We're grinding corn today, my good Wind," he said, "so see that you give me a nice steady blow. I'm not as unreasonable as the skipper. I don't care whether you blow from the north, south, east, or west, as long as you blow. I can adjust my sails to suit your convenience. But if you don't blow at all, then I'll really be mad!"

"Here I come, here I come!" said the Wind. And the sails of the windmill began to turn.

"Clever wind!" said the miller.

"Oh, dear! Now I have to lie low again," said the Wind. He stopped blowing and the sails stopped turning.

"Lousy wind!" said the miller.

Thursday morning the little boy who was sick stood gazing out the window.

"What kind of wind are you today?" he asked.

"I'm an east wind," the Wind answered.

"Oh, please be kind and turn around," said the little boy. "I've been terribly sick, and the doctor won't let me go out if the wind's from the east. I'd so love to go out. I haven't been in the forest all year—I haven't even used the lovely bow and arrow I got for my birthday. Please be kind, dear Wind. You surely won't refuse a poor, sick little boy!"

"I can't help you," wailed the Wind.

The little boy cried and stamped his feet. "I hate you! You're a bad, nasty wind," he said.

Friday morning the clergyman's wife was out in the field hanging her washing on the clothes-line.

"There's just the right amount of breeze," she said. "It's a perfect washing day. These will be dry by afternoon."

But by noon the wind had changed and turned

into a perfect gale. The posts creaked, the line snapped, the clothes were blown about and spread all over the ground. The clergyman's wife ran around frantically gathering them together.

"Lord, Lord—just look at them!" she said. "There's nothing else to do—we'll have to start the whole business over again. All on account of that devilish wind!"

"I couldn't help it!" shrieked the Wind.

By Saturday morning the Dandelion's seeds had ripened.

They waited patiently, each with its little parasol, for the wind to carry them out into the world. There were a great many of them. They were charming, and the Dandelion was so proud of them.

"It's nice to be pleased with one's children," she said. "I bloomed for their sakes, I nurtured them—now they must fend for themselves. Come, dear Wind, help me to launch them. If they all fell straight down and tried to take root in one spot, they'd be too crowded—they'd have no room to grow. That's why I've supplied them with little parachutes, so that they can drift some distance across the field. In this way the family spreads and will soon rule the world. So come, dear Wind, and carry them off. All we need is a gentle summer breeze."

"I can't. I can't," said the Wind. And he remained still. Absolutely still.

"You're a malicious, spiteful wind," said the Dandelion. "Yesterday you blew up such a storm that the clergyman's wife had all her washing ruined. And today you won't even deign to carry my tiny, featherweight children a few yards across the field. Shame, shame, shame on you!"

"I can't help it," sighed the Wind.

On Sunday morning the Wind lay sighing softly along the fence that bordered the forest. A little Mouse sat near him, licking her front paws and washing her whiskers.

"Poor Wind! Why do you keep on sighing?" she asked.

"Because I'm the most miserable creature on earth," answered the Wind.

"That's saying a lot," said the Mouse. "Of course, I scarcely know you. I'm so very small that I live close to the ground, so you usually pass above my head. But recently I heard some very nice things said about you."

"Someone spoke well of me?" asked the Wind. "Who was it? Do hurry up and tell me!"

"It was the poet," said the Mouse. "He sat here with his sweetheart reading poetry to her—poetry he'd written about you."

"Oh, the poet!" said the Wind dejectedly. "Well? What did the poetry say?"

"It said that you were warm and gentle—that you fanned her cheeks and played with her curls," said the Mouse.

"Yes, I daresay!" said the Wind. "But only the other day he was complaining that I'd mussed up her hair and made her nose red."

"And then there was something about how proudly, how superbly you swept over the sea," said the Mouse, "lashing the water into great waves with white foam on their crests. He said he could think of nothing more beautiful than that."

"The day before yesterday he went out for a sail," said the Wind, "got seasick, threw up, and hadn't a good word to say for me! No—he's no better than the rest of them."

"Well, if they're all against you, there must be something wrong with you," said the Mouse.

"Lord, yes—I suppose so. Lord, oh, Lord!" said the Wind. And he went on sighing and groaning. It was downright pitiful.

"Why not tell me all about it?" said the Mouse. "It sometimes helps a little. And, as you know, I'm quite unprejudiced. You've never harmed me, nor have you done me any good."

"I'm the most unfortunate creature in the world," said the Wind. "People imagine that I have great power—they ask me to do this, they beg me to do that—when the truth is, I'm nothing but a wretched slave bound to obey my master's slightest whim. I can do nothing on my own account."

"That's saying a lot," said the Mouse. "That would never have occurred to me."

"And yet it's the simple truth," said the Wind. "I get bawled out every day for running my master's errands."

"Who is your master?" asked the Mouse.

"My master is the Sun," said the Wind. "He's responsible for any harm I do, but I get all the blame."

"Explain," said the Mouse.

"It's easily explained," said the Wind. "As you see, I lie here quietly, harming no one, nothing, not even a cat—"

"Very kind of you," said the Mouse, "but you may as well know I shouldn't mind if you harmed a cat or two."

"It's not a question of kind or not kind," said the Wind. "I can do nothing on my own account. Listen to this: If the Sun decides to blaze down full force on some place in the east, I must instantly blow from the west—become a west wind whether I like it or not."

"I don't follow you," said the Mouse.

"Don't you see?" said the Wind. "The air the Sun has warmed rises—warm air always rises, since it's lighter than cold air."

The Mouse, who didn't understand a word, said in an offended tone, "It makes no difference to me—"

"But it does to me," said the Wind. "There's a vacuum where that warm air was—and so, right away, it's 'Hurry up, Wind! Bring in the cool air!' So if I'm lying still I have to dash off, or if I've been blowing from the east, I have to veer around instantly and blow from the west."

"I see," said the Mouse. "So that's how it is—you just have to obey."

"Exactly," said the Wind. "I never know which way I'm to blow till I receive my orders. And if I lie still, those who depend on me get mad and wonder what's become of me. If I'm ordered to blow from the west, I get nothing but curses from those who want me to blow from the east."

"It can't be much fun," said the Mouse.

"It's awful!" said the Wind. "You see, there are times when the Sun, without warning, suddenly decides to shine somewhere quite unexpectedly—and shine with great intensity. I have to dash away like a mad thing to get there in time to cool things off. That's when I turn into a storm. I sweep over land and sea, sometimes in my haste uprooting trees, blowing tiles off the roofs of houses, and even sinking ships. Then there's a great to-do about my wickedness. I'm blamed for every disaster that occurs. And it's really not my fault at all."

"I grant you that *is* a bit hard," said the Mouse.

"The Sun should be blamed, not you."

"That's just it," said the Wind. "But people glorify the Sun. They worship him."

"You should get someone to explain all this to them," said the Mouse.

"Who, for instance?" asked the Wind.

"You should have a talk with the poet," said the Mouse.

"A fat lot of good that'd do," said the Wind. "He cares nothing for facts. He wants subjects for poems and arranges things accordingly. You can hardly blame him for that—it's his business. He likes to picture me as pleasant, mild, and gentle. Or else as a high and mighty lord, arrogant and ruthless. If he knew me to be just a poor slave whipped from one end of the world to the other, subject to my master's every whim—how could he make a poem out of that?"

The Mouse looked thoughtful. "There may be something in that," she said.

"Look," said the Wind, "they're coming out of church. Just listen to what they say—then you'll know I don't exaggerate."

The Wind subsided along the fence, and the Mouse peeped out from under a dock leaf to watch them go by.

First came the clergyman's wife with the mother of the little boy who was sick. Next the skipper, then the miller and several other people.

"How's your little boy getting on?" asked the clergyman's wife.

"Thank you," said the mother, "he's a little better, but it's a slow business. We'd hoped to let him go out for a bit, but there was such a sharp wind we didn't dare."

"Yes! That wind—that wind! Dreadful!" said the clergyman's wife. "Can you imagine? Friday morning I hung out all my wash in the meadow. It was a perfect washing day, a mild breeze—just right for drying clothes, you know. Then, suddenly, this terrible gale blew up and ruined everything. We had to do the whole wash over again. All on account of that abominable wind!"

"I'm sorry to be late in getting your flour to you," said the miller to the farmer, "but I couldn't help it. It's not my fault, it's the wind's. You just couldn't depend on it from one hour to the next."

"The wind is the most unpredictable brute in the world," said the skipper. "If you want it to blow from the east, ten to one it'll blow from the west. If you need a good stiff breeze, you're sure to get a calm. But if it's a calm you want, there's bound to be a storm."

And they all walked on down the path.

"Those are true words," said the Apple Tree. "On Tuesday that wicked wind took all my lovely blossoms."

"It's true. The wind is a wicked monster," said the Dandelion. "It refused to launch my seeds Saturday morning."

"Did you hear?" asked the Wind.

"I heard," said the Mouse, "and I pity you with all my heart."

"And that's not the worst of it," said the Wind. "I've told you of my tragic fate, so you know that I am not responsible for the harm I do, but I must patiently accept the blame for my master's doings. Then would it surprise you to know that I sometimes give way to despair?"

"Not in the least," said the Mouse. "I'm surprised you can put up with it at all."

"I'm glad to hear you say that," said the Wind. "I do give way sometimes. The misery and injustice of my lot torments me so that I go roaring over the ocean, screaming through the rigging, howling down the chimneys, and whining through every crack and crevice. Do you know what they say then?"

"No. What?" said the Mouse.

"They say, 'Listen to the shriek of that terrible wind! . . . How awful that wind is, roaring out there! . . . That horrid wind howling in the chimney—so eerie!' "

"Poor Wind," said the Mouse.

The Wind said nothing more—only went on sighing deeply.

The Mouse didn't say anything either; she could think of no way to comfort him.

Suddenly there was a stir in the air.

The Wind roused himself. "Halloo-oo!" he shouted. "Where? From the south? Right! I'm coming—I'm coming!"

And he dashed off with such violence that the little Mouse was whirled around and around till she was so dizzy she could hardly find her way back to

her hole. When she finally reached it, she was quivering with rage.

"Disgusting, loathsome wind!" she cried. "Here I sat listening patiently to all his nonsense, and he plays this brutal trick on me. Whoever heard of such ingratitude?"

# The Queen Bee

It was spring, and the farmer opened up his beehive.

"Out you go!" he said to the bees. "The sun's shining, the trees are all in bud, flowers are popping up everywhere—spring's here at last! Now get to work, and see that you gather a whole lot of honey for me to take to market in the autumn. These are hard times for the farmer, and every little counts."

"A lot we care about your farming," murmured the bees.

But just the same, they flew out gladly. They'd been cooped up in the hive all winter and longed for a breath of fresh air. They hummed and they buzzed as they stretched their legs and tried their wings. There were many hundreds of them. They swarmed out. Then some settled on the roof of the hive, some flew toward the nearest flowers and bushes, and others crawled along the ground.

Last of all came the Queen Bee.

She was larger than the rest, and it was she who ruled over the hive.

"No more dawdling, children," she said. "Let's get busy! A respectable bee is never idle. She attacks her job with a will and makes the best use of her time."

She divided the bees into companies and gave each company its special task.

The first company went off to gather nectar from the flowers, which they then converted into honey. Another company collected pollen, to be kneaded into bee-bread. The last company of all was made up of the very youngest bees, who had never been put to work before. "What are *we* to do?" they asked.

"You? You're to sweat, of course!" cried the Queen. "Now then, get down to it!"

So they sweated away to the best of their ability; lovely yellow wax oozed out of their bodies.

"Very good!" said the Queen. "Now we can begin to build."

So the older bees took the wax and began building a quantity of small, hexagonal cells, each one fitted tightly against the others. While they were busy building, other bees kept flying in with honey and pollen, which they laid at the Queen's feet.

"Now you can start kneading the dough," she

said. "And be sure to add a little honey—it makes the bread taste better."

So they kneaded away, making lovely little loaves of bee-bread that they stored in some of the cells, while they filled others with pure honey.

"We must build more cells!" cried the Queen. And the young bees sweated wax for all they were worth, while the old bees went on building.

"Now it's time for me to start *my* work," said the Queen. And she heaved a great sigh, for her task was the most strenuous of all.

She settled down in the center of the hive and began laying eggs. She laid great heaps of them, and the nurse bees were kept busy picking them up one by one and depositing them in the new cells. Each egg had its own little compartment. When they were all disposed of, the Queen gave orders that doors should be fitted to each cell and kept tightly sealed.

"Excellent," she said when this had been done. "Now build me ten additional cells—and these must be more spacious."

The bees hurriedly obeyed. The Queen then laid ten exquisite eggs, one for each of the larger cells, and the doors were sealed upon them.

Each day the bees flew in and out, collecting honey and pollen. Toward evening, when their work was over, they couldn't resist opening the cell doors just a tiny crack to see how the eggs were getting on.

"Look out!" said the Queen one day. "Here they come!"

All at once the eggs burst open, and in each cell lay a sweet little baby grub.

The young bees looked at them curiously. "What funny little things!" they said. "Why, they've no eyes, and where are their legs and wings?"

"They are grubs," said the Queen. "You looked just like that—and not so long ago either! One has to be a grub before one can be a bee. Give them something to eat—quick, now!"

The bees were kept busy feeding the young grubs, but they didn't give the same food to all of them. The occupants of the ten larger cells were not only given all the bee-bread they could eat but were served large portions of honey as well. "They are the princesses," said the Queen, "and must have special treatment. Those others are just working bees; you can afford to skimp on them. They must just put up with what they get."

So the poor little things were given tiny pieces of bee-bread and nothing else. No matter how hungry they were, they had to be content with that.

In one of the little hexagonal cells adjoining the princesses' apartments lay a particularly tiny grub. She had only just emerged from her egg—she was the youngest of them all. She couldn't see, but she could hear quite distinctly, and she listened to the grown-up bees talking outside her cell. She lay there very quietly, thinking her own thoughts.

"I could certainly do with a bit more to eat," she said to herself and banged on her door. "I want some more to eat!" she called out.

"You've had quite enough for today," answered the old nurse bee who was on guard in the passage outside.

"But I'm hungry!" shouted the little grublet. "And I want to be moved into one of the princesses' cells—I feel cramped in here."

"Well! Listen to Her Highness!" mocked the old nurse bee. "Who do you think you are? Who are *you* to make demands? You were born to slave with the rest of us. You're just an ordinary worker, my dear, and you'll never be anything else."

"Oh, yes, I shall," said the grublet. "I shall be Queen—you'll see!" And she thumped on her door again.

The old nurse bee didn't even deign to answer. She went on with her work, tending to the other grubs. From all sides they were calling out, begging for more food. The little grublet heard them and thought to herself, "It's all wrong that we should be starved like this."

She knew that one of the princesses lay in a cell adjoining hers. She'd often heard her screaming for more honey, and she always got it too—the nurse bees never refused her anything. They always obeyed her promptly. The little grublet decided to appeal to her. She banged on the wall and called out, "Let me come in there with you and share some of your honey. I'm starving to death in here, and I'm just as good as you are!"

But the princess answered angrily, "Just you wait till I become Queen. I shan't forget your impudence."

No sooner had she said this than one of the other princesses shouted, *"You* won't be Queen—I shall!"

Then another one joined in, and then another, until they were all shouting at once, *"I* shall be Queen! *I* shall! *I! I! I!"* And they banged on the walls of their apartments and kept on yelling till the noise was positively deafening.

The old nurse bee came running. "What do Your Highnesses wish?" she asked, with much bowing and scraping.

"More honey!" they shrieked. "But I must be served first," cried one. "No, no! *I* must! *I* must! *I'm* to be the Queen!" And the shouting started all over again.

The old nurse bee ran off as fast as her six old legs could carry her, and she and her assistants soon returned, dragging with them a great quantity of honey, which they crammed down the throats of the angry little princesses. In this way they succeeded in quieting them, and they were soon fast asleep.

But the little grublet couldn't get to sleep. She lay awake thinking of all she had heard. She longed for some of that honey, and pretty soon she started pounding on her door again.

"I want some honey too!" she called out. "I'm

just as good as they are. I won't stand this any longer!"

The old nurse bee tried to hush her up. "Will you be quiet, you little wretch?" she said. "Here comes the Queen!"

And, sure enough, at that very moment the Queen came slowly down the passage toward the princesses' apartments. "I wish to be alone. Leave me!" she said, and the old nurse bee hurried off.

For a long time there was silence. Then the little grublet heard the Queen whispering to herself. "They're lying in there asleep, all those fine princesses," she said. "They eat and they sleep, and each day they get larger and stronger. Soon they'll be full-grown; then they'll come out of their cells and my reign will be over. The bees will want a new Queen, one younger and more beautiful than I am, and I'll be turned out in disgrace. Well—I won't stand for that. Tomorrow I shall kill these fine princesses—kill every one of them. Then I can go on reigning till I die."

The little grublet heard the Queen creep softly away.

"What a dreadful thing!" she thought. "The prin-

cesses may be proud and haughty—and they were certainly mean to me—but, still, I don't think they should be murdered. I'd better report this to that old grumble-bee out there."

So she banged on her door again, and the old nurse bee came running. This time she was really angry. She opened the grublet's door a crack and growled at her in her most ferocious voice, "See here, my girl. I warn you, if I hear one more word out of you I'll report you to the Queen!"

As she started to close the door, the grublet called out, "No! Wait! Listen to me—it's important!" Then she told the old nurse bee about the Queen's wicked plan.

"Good gracious! Is this true?" cried the old nurse bee, fluttering her wings in horror. She didn't wait to hear any more, but hurried off to tell the others.

"She might have given me a little honey for my pains," said the little grublet. "But at least now I can go to sleep with a clear conscience."

The next evening when the Queen felt sure that all the bees had gone to rest, she crept stealthily toward the princesses' apartments. The little grublet heard her. "Oh, dear! Now she's going to murder them!" she thought, and she squeezed herself as close to the door as possible so as to hear all that went on. She heard the Queen softly—very softly—opening the door of the first princess's cell, and at that very moment the bees swarmed in on her from all sides, seized her by the legs and the wings, and dragged her away.

"What's the meaning of this?" shouted the Queen. "Is this a revolution?"

"By no means, Your Majesty," answered the bees respectfully. "But we know of your plan to kill the princesses, and you can't be allowed to do this. What would happen to us in the autumn when Your Majesty dies?"

"Let me go!" shrieked the Queen as she tried to free herself. "Remember, I'm still Queen—I can still do as I choose! And what makes you think I shall die in the autumn?"

But the bees held her fast and dragged her right out of the hive. There they let her go. She shook her wings furiously at them and said, "Disloyal, rebellious subjects! I no longer wish to rule over you—I consider you unworthy. I refuse to stay here another moment. I shall go away and start another hive. Who will follow me?"

A few of the older bees, who had been grubs when the Queen was only a princess, decided to go with her—and shortly afterward they flew away.

"Here we are without a Queen," said the bees. "Now we must take especially good care of our princesses." So they stuffed them with honey from morning till night, and they grew fat and strong, and quarrelsome, and more self-important every day.

But no one gave a thought to the little grublet.

One morning the doors of the princesses' apartments flew open, and they emerged as full-grown, beautiful young Queens. The other bees gathered round and gazed at them with wonder and admiration. "How beautiful they are!" they exclaimed. "It's quite impossible to say which is the loveliest."

*"I* am, of course!" shouted one of the princesses.

"I think you are mistaken," said another, and she jabbed at the first one with her stinger.

"Are you both crazy?" cried a third. *"I'm* much more beautiful than either of *you!"*

Then they all started screaming at each other. At last they began to fight, and they certainly fought with a vengeance. Some of the bees tried to stop them, but the old nurse bee cried out, "Let them fight! Then we'll find out who is strongest and choose her for our Queen. After all, we can't have more than one."

So the bees formed a ring and watched the battle. It was long and fierce. Bits of legs and torn wings hurtled through the air, and after a while eight of the princesses lay on the ground stone dead. The two survivors still kept up the struggle. One had no wings left, and the other had only four legs instead of six.

"Whichever one wins, we'll have a sorry-looking Queen!" said one of the bees. "We'd have done better to keep the old one."

But she needn't have worried, for just as she said this, the two remaining princesses stung each other with such vigor that they both fell down dead.

"Now we have no Queen at all!" cried the bees in dismay. "What shall we do? What shall we do? Who will guide us? Who will rule over us?" They buzzed and they hummed in fear and confusion. The hive was in a state of chaos.

One of the oldest and wisest of the bees decided to call a conference. She gathered the elders of the hive around her, and they discussed at great length various ways of solving the problem, but they could come to no agreement.

At last the old nurse bee managed to make herself heard above the clash of argument. "I know exactly what to do," she cried. "Just listen to me and follow my advice." When they had quieted down, she continued, "I can remember a long time ago the same thing happening here in this very hive. I was a grub at the time, and from my cell I heard all that went on. The old Queen had gone away, and the princesses fought each other until they all lay dead—it was precisely the situation we face now. At that time it was decided to transfer an ordinary grub into one of the dead princesses' apartments and treat it as though it had been born a princess. It was given all it could eat of the very finest honey, and it grew up to be an exceptionally good and beautiful Queen. I remember it all very clearly. I kept wondering at the time why they hadn't chosen me! But they didn't, so that's neither here nor there. I should like to suggest that we proceed in the same way."

The old nurse bee was warmly applauded, and her suggestion was immediately adopted. The bees started off to choose a grub at once.

"Just a moment!" the old nurse bee called out. "I can be of help to you in this—take me along. The grub you choose must be among the very youngest. She must be given as much time as possible to adjust to her new position. When you've been brought up as a common working bee, it can't be so easy to get used to the thought of wearing a crown."

The bees all agreed that this was highly sensible, and the old nurse bee continued, "There's a tiny little grub—the youngest one of all—in a cell adjoining the princesses' apartments. She must have learned a lot from overhearing their elegant and cultivated speech. I myself have noticed that she has a lot of character, and I think we owe her special consideration, for it was she who told me of the old Queen's wicked plan. Let us choose her!"

So all the bees went in a solemn procession to the humble, narrow cell where the little grublet lay. The old nurse bee knocked politely at her door, cautiously opened it, and told her she had just been chosen for their Queen. At first the grublet could scarcely believe it, but when she found herself being carried with great care and ceremony into one of the spacious apartments, and when the bees started bringing her all the honey she could eat, she realized it was true.

"So, old grumble-bee—I'm Queen after all!" she called out. "I told you I would be, but you wouldn't believe it!"

The old nurse bee curtsied respectfully. "I hope Your Majesty will overlook any rude remarks I may have made," she said humbly.

"I forgive you," answered the new-baked princess. "Just fetch me some more honey!"

Not long afterward, the grublet was full-grown and came out of her chamber as large and beautiful as the bees could well have wished. And there was no doubt that she knew how to give orders.

"Off with you!" she cried. "We must have a lot more honey for the winter. And you, over there, must sweat much more wax. I'm adding a new wing to the hive. In future the princesses will live there.

It's very unpleasant for them to be so near the common grubs."

"Well, well—listen to her!" murmured the older bees, exchanging amused glances.

"She must surely *always* have been a Queen, even in her egg!" exclaimed one of the young bees admiringly.

"No," said the old nurse bee. "But she certainly always had queenly thoughts. Sometimes that's even better."

## *About the Translator*

Eva Le Gallienne, whose name is known and respected throughout the world of dramatic arts, was born in London. Her father was a well-known author, and her mother was a Danish journalist who as a child sat on Hans Christian Andersen's lap when he told fairy tales to her class.

Miss Le Gallienne was educated in Paris and made her stage debut in London. Actor, director, and translator, she has translated seven of Ibsen's plays into English and has appeared in plays by Shakespeare, Ibsen, and many contemporary dramatists. Most recently she starred in the Broadway production of *The Royal Family,* and she has just completed work in a new motion picture.

Eva Le Gallienne's previous publications include translations of several Hans Christian Andersen tales, as well as two autobiographical books, *At 33* and *With a Quiet Heart,* and a book for children, *Flossie and Bossie.* She now lives in Weston, Connecticut.

## *About the Illustrator*

Bill Woodman is a free-lance cartoonist whose works have appeared in books and several magazines, including the *New Yorker.* He has recently written and illustrated another children's book, *Whose Birthday Is It?* Mr. Woodman lives in New York City with his wife and two children.